THERE IS *Hope* WITHIN

BARBARA BAILEY

This literary work is a historical fiction. Names, characters, places, and incidents have been changed to fit this genre.

Printed in the United States of America

Library of Congress Cataloging – in Publication Data

Editorial Assistance:
Jabez Books Writers' Agency
(A Division of Clark's Consultant Group)
www.clarksconsultantgroup.com

ISBN 978-0-9839248-1-4

Unless otherwise indicated, all scripture references are from the Holy Bible, King James Version.

Acknowledgements

- To my grandmother, who is dear to my heart and taught me to always trust in God where all hope originates.
- To my mother, who is looking down from heaven with a smile.
- To my children and grandchildren, the precious gifts from God that I will cherish forever.
- To my sisters, who have always been there for me standing in the gap with their prayers and love.
- Special thanks to Dr. Shirley Clark and Jabez Books Writer's Agency for all their help in the publication of this book.

Table of Contents

Introduction

The Definition of Hope

What is hope? According to Dictionary.com, hope is the feeling that what is wanted can be achieved or that something will turn out for the best; to look forward to with desire and reasonable confidence.

As stated by Dr. Jennifer Cheavens, Assistant Psychology Professor at Ohio State University, "If you feel you know how to get what you want out of life, and you have that desire to make that happen, then you have hope."

The theological virtue of hope is defined as the desire and search for a future good, difficult but not impossible to attain with God's help (Dictionary by Farlex).

"For we are saved by hope: but hope that is seen is not hope: for what a man seeth, why doth he yet hope for? But if we hope for that we see not, then do we with patience wait for it" (Romans 8: 24-25).

"Be of good courage, and He shall strengthen your heart, all ye that hope in the Lord" (Psalms 31:24).

Chapter 1

The Awakening

There is an element within everyone where hope can be ignited. To know God and His magnificent love for us gives us the ability to have faith; and where there is faith, there is hope.

The story that I am about to unfold on the pages in this book is a story of hope; and hopefully, it will generate hope within your life.

The setting of this story takes place in the city of Dallas in the year of 1996. Mary Jackson (mother) tells the story as seen through her eyes and from information received in letters from her son, James Jackson.

James grew up to be an intelligent young man, yet he still struggled with the ability to see any future or hope in his life. The younger of two siblings, James always felt left out and that he had to compete with his brother and sister.

Today was just like any other ordinary day for James as he approached the probation office that he visited once a week, but the next few minutes of his life became a nightmare.

"Good morning," James spoke as he entered the office.

"Good morning," replied Ms. Jacobs, the probation officer.

Ms. Jacobs, a short stout lady with a very nice personality, was always friendly but strict. James noticed a different atmosphere in the office than previous visits. There were two policemen also standing in the room which was unusual.

"James, I'm sorry, but you will have to go with these officers, because you have not paid anything on the probation fees in six months," said Ms. Jacobs.

"The Probation Director informed me this morning that failure to pay your fees for this length of time was unacceptable."

After the officers placed the handcuffs on James, he was lost for words and knew that Ms. Jacobs was telling the truth. All he could do was obey the officers, even though running seemed like a good idea. At this point, James knew this was it; time had caught up with him.

As James was driven to his gilded cage, it seemed like the longest ride he had ever taken to a place he did not want to go. After the booking, he was placed in a cell with other inmates. The walls seemed to be closing in; eyes staring at him, and an unfamiliar atmosphere were all around him. Was this a dream? James pinched himself to be sure before calling his mom.

James, 25 years old, is a small frame, handsome, shy, but bold young man who always proved himself to be a leader among his friends. Because he was left-handed since birth, his mother, Mary, looked upon him as her special blessed child.

James' mother from his early childhood could sense that he would require lots of attention. When James was four years old, he placed his sister's doll on the kitchen stove to watch it burn. He enjoyed exploring things and watching the outcome, but never anticipated the danger of it.

In grade school, James was classified as the "class clown" by his teachers. He could never stay focused on school work and did not want his classmates to focus either. James was a daydreamer and his mind was always thinking of things to get into and places to go.

James hesitated before picking up the phone because he knew how this was going to upset his mom. On the other hand, he knew that his mom always seemed to make things right no matter what. However, his father, David, was the exact opposite. James' father was not as understanding as his mother, and he also did not want to take the chance of being fussed or screamed at, so he knew definitely not to call him.

As well, their relationship was strained and he did not feel comfortable talking with his father. Growing up with his father always gave James a sense of fright and uneasiness due to his tough and hostile manner.

James also remembered how strict his father was during his childhood years and the many times he and his siblings were not allowed to go outside and play with their neighborhood friends because of this. They would have to cleanup and do other menial chores. As well as, they could not sleep late when school was out or on the weekends. It seemed as though they always had to work and keep busy around the house....no play time.

James had a difficult time most of his life, however, this was not because of how his father disciplined them, but it was mainly due to some of the poor choices he made in life. James was constantly making decisions that rendered negative outcomes in his life.

But despite all of this, when it came to James' siblings, he always looked up to them, especially his older brother, John, who was two years older, and wanted to be like him. John is tall, slender, good looking, well groomed and enjoys dressing according to the GQ magazine for men. John is very artistic and possesses architectural skills. John is also an entrepreneur, married and has four children.

James was also close to his sister, Sarah, who was one year older. Sarah, a tall very confident pretty young lady, has a very unique style and gift for decorating and writing.

Sarah chose to have a loving family life with a wonderful husband and four beautiful girls. In high school Sarah wanted to become a fashion model, but she forfeited this dream to become a loving wife and mother.

John and Sarah have always been supportive of James, but he never felt that he could ever become as successful financially and mentally as they were. He desired to have a nice home, car and family as his siblings, but had no clue where to begin to acquire these things; or maybe he did know, but just did not want to take the initiative to go after them.

Six months ago, James was found guilty of an assault charge, and since it was his first offense, he was given probation. That whole scene was a nightmare in itself. Now James is about to face another situation relating to his first assault charge and he is desperately looking for help and some hope.

Unlocking the door to her house, Mary dropped her keys on the table and ran to catch the phone. She quickly scanned the caller ID just in case it was one of those pesky telemarketers. Her heart skipped a beat when she read the caller ID — "Dallas County Jail." Mary hurriedly picked up the phone and heard a recorded message.

"Will you accept a call from James Jackson?"

"Yes, yes!" she shouted into the receiver.

"Mama," James said in a frightened voice.

"I'm in jail!!!"

Time seemed to stop for Mary.

"What do you mean, in jail?" she asked.

"I went to my regular probation sessions and the cops were waiting for me."

"What did they arrest you for, son?"

"I-I didn't pay my probation fees and have not paid them for a while now. My probation officer agreed to work with me until I found a job, but now everything has turned sour. Mama, I will go before the judge tomorrow who will assign me a court date and I'll call you when I find out."

James kept waiting for someone to wake him up from this terrible dream, but each passing minute became an unfortunate reality. He knew without a shadow of a doubt that this incident was the beginning of something that frightened him to death.

"Why was this happening?" James thought to himself.

"It seems as though there is always something going wrong with my life."

As Mary hung up the phone, she knew what the next step to take. James' father needed to be contacted. First of all, she had to get her composure together and calm herself down.

David and Mary had been divorced now for eight years following a twenty year marriage. Mary worked downtown as an Accounting Manager and David owned a small travel agency in North Dallas.

Still partially in shock, Mary dialed the number.

"Hello," David answered loudly as he always did due to a hearing defect from childhood.

"Hello, how are you doing?" asked Mary.

"Oh, I'm fine, what's wrong?" David seemed to sense the shaking in her voice.

"James is in jail for not paying his probation fees."

"What!" shouted David? "Can we bail him out on bond?"

"Not until the judge sets a court date," answered Mary.

"How long will that take?"

"I'm not sure David, probably sometime tomorrow," replied Mary.

"I'll try to contact my friend's attorney just in case James needs representation," David shouted.

After she hung up the phone, Mary decided to contact the county jail for any updated information about James' case. They told her that court was set for 9:00 A.M. in the morning. Mary informed David of the news and they agreed to ride together to the court hearing.

Mary began to think about her son's safety as she considered his incarceration state. The terrible feeling she had at that time, as a mother, unable to do anything was unexplainable. Mary knew that prayer was the only solution to calming her nerves. As she began to pray to God, the only thing that Mary could think of ---this must be a dream, but it felt so real.

Her mind took her back to James' childhood days when he was about seven years old. Mary received a phone call from school that James had fallen off the monkey bar on the playground and was hurt. If it was not for David with his strong spirit, Mary would not have made it through that ordeal. She remembers how swollen James' lip and face were when they picked him up from school. Despite the way his injury looked, it was not as serious as it appeared according to the doctor who examined him.

Then there was the time when James was about nine years old and he was hit in the eye by a baseball and a blood vessel burst.

Through it all, James survived those incidents, along with several others. But Mary was somewhat frightened about the mess he was in today as a young man. Mary wanted hope for all her children, but it always seemed that James was constantly experiencing trouble. Was there still hope for her baby son to survive this terrible ordeal that has fallen upon him?

Chapter 2

The Courtroom

As they entered the court house, David and Mary were both silent. David's 5'11" stature was always so tall and strong. Mary was small and petite, standing at 5'2", with a very sassy walk. David never showed much emotion until now. He was very nervous, but tried to remain calm around Mary.

"Mary, I talked with an attorney last night who is going to meet us here. His legal fee is $1000, $250 down payment and the balance after the trial."

Mary was partly listening to David because her mind was focused on the outcome of the trial. They sat outside the courtroom until the session began. About five minutes before court was scheduled to start, Mary and David were approached by a very stout middle aged gentleman in an old dingy looking gray suit.

"Are you the Jacksons?"

David and Mary rose to their feet to greet him. "Yes," they replied.

"I am Ross Miller, the defense attorney you spoke with last night."

Smelling like cheap booze, Mr. Miller asked for the down payment before they entered the courtroom. David handed him a check for $250. Mr. Miller informed David and Mary that he picked up James' file from the court records and everything would be fine. Mary's heart sank to her stomach as she thought in her mind.

"Lord, is this the man that is representing my child?"

As they entered the courtroom, an older gentleman with eyes of vengeance and a young lady with short red hair and a loose disposition were seated in the back, which later were identified as the plaintiff and her father from James' previous case six months ago. Mr. Miller opened his briefcase to review the files of the case. Minutes later the District Attorney, a young arrogant slender woman with dark brown hair, entered the courtroom with an attitude of winning the case against James. The Judge, a very tall gray-haired man with dark rimmed eye glasses, entered to take his seat. Finally, James was escorted in and ordered to take the stand. This case would be decided by the Judge in this situation.

The trial by judge was in session after James' conviction six month ago. At that time he was sentenced to two years probation. Now, six months later of failing to pay probation fees, he was back in court again. The nervousness on James' face was evident as the District Attorney began to speak. Mary knew her child and she could feel that James was desperately crying out for help by his expressions and the trembling in his voice.

"Mr. Jackson you are on trial today for probation violation. Therefore, your previous case will be revisited and the Judge will make the final decision, said Linda Ham, the prosecutor. You were charged with assaulting Anita Fox, the plaintiff. Can you tell us what happened the night of September 21, 1996?"

James remembered every detail of that day as if it happened yesterday. Time seemed to stand still as the incident played back in his head. If he had only waited and invited the young lady to meet his mom first, maybe this chapter in his life would not be happening today. James always had a habit of introducing a lady friend to his mom to get her opinion since mothers tend to have that 'mother wit' and can sense any danger ahead of time for her children. Even though James would make his own decisions, most of the time, he always valued his mother's advice. This is the only time that Mary can remember James not bringing a young lady to meet his mother and get her approval.

Approaching the front door of the plaintiff's apartment to avoid a senseless brawl over a cell phone call he received while they ate dinner, James was ready to go.

"I'm leaving. This dinner date was a mistake."

James thought back how his best friend, Matt, introduced him to Anita. He began to regret that he ever met her and wanted this whole incident to be just a terrible dream.

"Oh, now it's a mistake after you've eaten my food and have taken advantage of my kindness," screamed Anita angrily.

"I knew you were a cheater when we met. Before you go anywhere, you are going to pay back the money that I spent on dinner and wine, and most of all my time."

"I told you when we met that my money was low due to demanding obligations," James shouted.

"That's no excuse," Anita blurted out, as she began hitting James on his back. "You have wasted my time and money."

"Calm down, Anita. You are acting like a crazy woman," James implied as he held her arms to prevent any further action from her. As James released the grip he had on Anita, she fell backwards and hit the floor. It was an accident.

"Mr. Jackson, Mr. Jackson would you please answer the question," repeated the prosecutor.

James snapped back to reality and responded suddenly.

"We were arguing about a phone call that I received on my cell and then the issue of money came up," stated James.

"Anita began hitting me and to protect myself, I held both of her arms. When I let go of her and started to walk away; she grabbed my shirt from behind in an attempt to prevent me from leaving. I turned around and held her arms again as she continued to struggle. At that moment, I let go; Anita lost her balance and fell to the floor. That is when she threatened to call the police and tell them that I had a gun."

"Isn't it true Mr. Jackson that you pushed the plaintiff down?" inquired the prosecutor.

"No I did not," replied James.

"Mr. Jackson you were placed on probation six months ago because the court found you guilty of an attempted assault charge against Miss Fox. Due to no prior trouble with the law you did not have to serve any time. Now can you tell the court today why you have not paid your probation fees?"

"I have been unable to find work due to the felony charge on my record, but I've never missed the monthly probation meetings. I informed my probation officer that I could not pay the fees and she told me to just pay them when I could."

James thought back in his mind about the opportunity he had to work with his father to at least pay the fees, but failed to do so.

"Mr. Jackson you have violated the probation laws of the State of Texas. No further questions," stated the prosecutor.

Finally, Mr. Ross approached the stand. David and Mary squirmed in their seats as Mr. Ross began to question James.

"Mr. Jackson, did you intentionally push the plaintiff down to harm her?"

"No sir," replied James.

"Mr. Jackson, were you aware that failure to pay your probation fees would result in a warrant for your arrest?" Mr. Ross asked.

"No sir," James answered.

"Are you willing to work out a payment plan to pay off the probation fees?" said Mr. Ross.

"Yes sir," James replied.

"No further questions," stated Mr. Ross.

The Judge and prosecutor looked stunned and so did David and Mary. What kind of defense was that -- just three very quick questions to the defendant? At that time Mary felt a lump in her throat and David was on the edge of his seat. The consequences were looking very slim for James.

Miss Ham stepped forward and gave her closing statement to Judge Lee.

"Your Honor, I recommend that Mr. Jackson be sent to a prison farm at a correctional facility for 24 months to help him learn the importance of obeying the laws of the State of Texas. I rest my case."

Mr. Ross came forth with his closing statement.

"Your Honor, I recommend that the defendant be allowed another chance to prove himself to the court and society. I request an additional 12 month probation sentence along with a payment plan to pay past due probation fees and community service. I rest my case."

Judge Lee requested a 30 minute recess to review the documents in front of him and the notes he jotted down during the trial.

As he returned to the bench, Judge Lee asked James to stand up.

"Mr. Jackson, I have made my decision. You were given a second chance when the court placed you on probation six months ago, but you did not comply with the Texas laws by failing to pay the assigned probation fees. Therefore, James Jackson, you are hereby sentenced to 18 months at the Lade Knox Farm prison facility located in Houston, Texas. This trial is now adjourned."

James was escorted out of the courtroom by two officers. He never looked in the direction of his parents. Mary was so stunned, she could not speak and the tears began to flow. David's first reaction was to grab his son and run, but the officers glanced once in his direction with a threatening look; all he could do was just sit in astonishment. Mary could only see her son being taken away to an unfamiliar place and it scared her to death.

James was driven to the farm by bus the next day. Mary did not know how she would survive this sudden storm in her life and David was lost for words.

Mary thought, "Was all <u>hope</u> gone for James?"

She is now a mother holding on while her son searches to find hope.

Chapter 3

Lade Knox Prison Farm
(The Lockup)

James' trip to the farm was the longest ride he had ever experienced. Sitting on the bus with 39 other men, he was not looking forward to this venture. He thought how quickly his life changed in a flash. No way he thought that one dinner date would change his life forever. What could he have done differently to prevent this from happening?

Everything was beginning to look like a nightmare.

Once they arrived at the prison farm each man was checked in one by one and given an identification number. James still could not believe that he would be stuck here for 18 months.

As he entered the first gate which shut immediately with a loud bang, there were two more gates to enter that shut the same way. Each gate was surrounded with a barb wire fence at least 20 feet high. The next entrance was to the main building. The prison cells were on floors three and above. Each cell was equipped with 20 beds all situated against the wall. James was told that he was actually at a holding facility which was not as dangerous as some of the hard core facilities. Still, just the fact that he was not able to go and do as he pleased was very frightening.

James was very hesitant about disclosing any information about his conviction to the inmates. When asked what he was in for, James always replied, "Attempted murder." He thought this would put fear in the inmates and they would stay away from him. If they asked for more information, James was ready for that because he always had a way with words. He was so dramatic growing up that his sister labeled him as 'the boy that cried wolf.' No one could ever tell if he was telling the truth or making it up.

After two weeks in Lade Knox, James befriended an older gentleman of Muslim faith, Abdul Aalee, who educated him about the not-so-pleasant prison life; such as, what to do and not to do, what to say and not to say. Abdul was doing time for the murder of his wife. He insisted that he was wrongly accused, but could not afford the proper legal counsel. Since there were no witnesses, he was convicted and was serving a life term.

As time progressed Abdul tried a few times to influence James to accept the Muslim faith. James' Christian beliefs that were instilled in him as a child would not permit him to think about changing to a different faith even in his present condition. He knew that God is a Spirit and Mohammad Allah was not God.

James quickly became accustomed to a very different style of living realizing that he would have to think quickly and do what was necessary to survive. James began to pray and hope for a miracle. He remembered, as a child, his father and mother's faith and trust in God.

The inmates' time schedule was very strict and demanding. They arose every morning at 5:00 A.M. to freshen up and eat breakfast before going to work in the field. On Sunday's, they had the option to attend church services. Following three months of field work, James was eligible to transfer to kitchen duty and was very elated about this as cited in his letter that he wrote to Mary.

Also, James would send a letter to his mother at least once a week because she insisted on it. That was their means of communication when she was not able to go and visit him. James would also send hand-made cards with poetry in them to Mary in his spare time. Mary did not realize James' gift of creativity and poetry until now.

James' letter to Mary explained that he was transferred to kitchen duty and he did not have to chop weeds that were taller than him anymore.

James continued to tell Mary in his letter about some of the things that were going on there, but refused to inform her of the dreadful untold incidents for fear that she would worry about his safety. James was counting down the months until his release.

Mary wrote encouraging letters to James weekly reminding him to trust God and know that He is able to protect and keep him safe there. This profound information was revealed to Mary by God Himself. After James departure to the prison farm, Mary was so heartbroken that it was difficult for her to function at work or perform any type of daily duties. Driving home from work one day, Mary was crying profusely and God spoke to her spirit with a calm voice.

"Why are you crying my dear, James is alright and I am watching over him. Have you forgotten that My Presence is everywhere and all power is in My Hands?"

"Trust Me on this one," spoke the Holy Spirit.

"I know what's best for James in this time and season of his life."

At that particular time, Mary knew without a shadow of doubt that God would do what He said. Mary began to realize that nothing just happens and everything happens for a reason.

Mary always tried to visit James at least twice a month to ensure that all was well with her son. But the impact was so disturbing to David emotionally that he was not able to visit James during his 18 month stay. He was very hurt and heartbroken from the terrible ordeal. David was always such a strong-willed father, and he did not want James to see him cry.

David loved James very much and could not accept that his youngest son was imprisoned behind bars like a criminal. Therefore, he would always rely on Mary to give him a report on James' condition. As long as David was sure that his son was fine, he did not feel that it was necessary to visit him. For James this was comforting as well. He did not want his father to visit him because he felt like a disappointment to him by his imprisonment.

On the other hand, James was always close to his mother and felt safe when she was around. God knew that Mary had to let go and let God to make it possible for James to become an independent young man. This is exactly what happened.

James' stay at the facility helped him become more independent and responsible. It quickened his awareness to fend for himself, and make the best decisions whenever necessary.

Time was really moving quickly. One year had passed and James continued to count down the days for the last six months that he would have to spend in that dreadful place.

During James' stay at the prison farm seemed like a lifetime and he began to wonder why this unfortunate thing happened to him. Finally, he began to read the Bible and watch some Christian TV.

All the inmates would gather around the television on Sunday to watch one of the well known Dallas ministers on TV. The pastor's encouraging words kept their eyes glued to the television set. James soon began to realize that everything happens for a reason and it's never too late to turn your life around.

Everything about James' life began to fall into place. He knew that the situation he was in resulted from bad choices. In this particular season of his life, James experienced life without freedom and he never wanted to go that route again.

He witnessed many fights and unforeseen acts among the inmates; some of them resulted in a bad end. James was very confident that God was watching over him and he had no fear.

As the release date grew nearer, James became happier and excited. He had a long list of things to do once he made it home. At the top of the list was — to find a job and get his life back on track. James thought of facing the world again as a free man would be a challenge, but he knew God was his only hope.

Chapter 4

The Release

t was finally time to go home. James packed his personal items all in one bag and along with $30, and a bus ticket that is given to each inmate upon release, and he started home to Dallas.

James' room and board became one of the halfway houses for 30 days which is the procedure of the Parole Board System. This setup did not bother James; he was now free.

Following the 30 days, James would stay with David and work with him until James could afford a place of his own. The Parole Board assigned James 12 months of parole in which he would have to report to a local office every month and pay parole fees. His driver's license will have to be renewed every year for the next 10 years. James knew that he did not want to make another mistake, and definitely did not want to go back to that type of environment. He was determined to never miss the parole appointments or fail to pay the parole fees.

During James' parole period, he managed to maintain all requirements as well as working on several odd jobs while continuing to work with his father. The parole period passed quickly, but James still faced other issues that he was facing prior to his stay at Lade Knox -- dealing with the felony on his record again, which prevented him from obtaining a good job and there was also a child support issue.

Before his prison stay, James was told that he was the father of a baby boy. James was excited and proud due to his desire to have a son. There was no doubt in his mind that he was the father even though his father insisted that he take a blood test.

James was sure, so he refused to follow his father's advice. James' time at Lade Knox cost him child support back pay and refusal of visitation rights by the mother of the baby once he was released. When James considered all of this, questions of doubt began to enter his mind once again.

"Will there ever be any <u>hope</u> for me? What is my purpose for being here and why are these issues in my life? Every time I try to advance forward, something always seems to pull me two steps backwards. I know that I've made some bad choices, but will I ever come out of this mess and be able to live a normal life?"

James decided to move in with Mary, his mother. At this point, he wanted to really work on getting his life together. He was not getting any younger. At times, because of his futile job searches, he became so discouraged and did not want to continue on in life.

When Mary became aware of James' feelings of depression, she sought out the only source that is able to do all things -- God. God reminded her of two scriptures as she sought Him:

"The thief cometh not but for to steal, and to kill, and to destroy; I am come that they might have life, and that they might have it more abundantly" (John 10:10).

Mary explained to James how the enemy desires to take us all out (destroy us) as well as steal our joy and hinder our blessings; but God has given us power over the enemy.

"Now unto him that is able to do exceeding abundantly above all that we ask or

think according to the power that worketh in us" (Ephesians 3:20). There is nothing too impossible for God and He can help us if we have the faith to use our spiritual weapons.

According to Bishop T.D. Jakes, a New York Times Best-Selling author, "Hopelessness is what makes people give up on life. They are convinced there's nothing beyond what they have experienced or seen. Hope keeps you going when the storms of life hit."

God knows all our thoughts and everything that we go through, and He is right there all the time just waiting on us to ask for His help.

Through Mary's encouragement, love and prayers, James began to see some positive things happen in his life. He began to see a reason to live and to seek God's destiny for his life. God began to open up doors and opportunities for James.

James became a member of the Bible teaching church where his mother attends. He also volunteered to work with the Prison Ministry.

Within two years, James met and married Jada, who he met at church. Jada is a tiny slender woman with a high strong and very outgoing personality.

James and Jada are trusting and believing in God for a long and successful marriage. They both realize that it will take working and praying together on one accord to accomplish the plan and purpose that God has destined for their lives.

Through the blessings of God, James is the CEO of a courier service and Jada owns a beauty shop. James and Jada still struggle from time to time with day to day issues in trying to resolve them; but they know that it is God's love, his mother's prayers and their love for each other that have kept their marriage together.

God knows that we all have issues, some more than others. But regardless of what we do, if we will acknowledge our problem(s), God will help us overcome.

It only took a little while for James to finally understand that life's issues don't always pick you, sometimes you choose them. If you want to survive, you can't give up and quit. The key to surviving is to know without a shadow of doubt that hope is always within our reach, and it is in Jesus Christ. He gives each of us the desire to hope.

Psalms 33:18 & 22 states – *"Behold, the eye of the Lord is upon them that fear him, upon them that hope in his mercy. Let thy mercy, O Lord, be upon us, according as we hope in thee."*

Through his experiences and struggles, James realized that we must always strive to keep a clear mind and have the inner ability to recognize the hope within. He also recognized, it is very important to stay focused, be obedient to God's Word, trust Him, have faith, and know that, where there is Faith and Love, there is always HOPE!

About the Author ──────────

Barbara Bailey, born in Austin, Texas and raised in Waco, Texas under the tutelage of her paternal grandmother with two sisters, has always been an avid book reader. As she began to enjoy reading more and more, Barbara developed the encouragement and desire to write, but the motivation was not quite there to complete the publication process. Reading, next to writing and music is one of her favorite passionate hobbies.

After her high school graduation, Barbara moved to Dallas and went on to graduate with a BBS and MBA in Finance. Barbara has two sons – Tyrone and Mark; one daughter – Valerie, and ten grandchildren. She worked most of her life in corporate America utilizing her skills and knowledge in the area of Finance and Accounting.

Following the layoff at her job, Barbara decided to pursue something that she became very passionate about over the years, but could not find the time to do it……writing. Through many prayers and reading several books, Barbara believes that writing is one of the many gifts God has given her. As the Holy Spirit provides the information and inspiration for her to write, she will continue to be obedient to the unction of His leading.

During her spare time, Barbara is a volunteer for Texas Offenders Reentry Initiative Program (TORI) and The Bishop's Choir at The Potter's House Church in Dallas, Texas. She is also an Aaron's Army Partner with Bishop T. D. Jakes Ministries and member of Greater Waco Interfaith Conference (GWIC) and the National Association of Professional Women (NAPW).

To order additional copies of
this book, please contact:

Barbara Bailey Enterprises
barbarabailey@prodigy.net
www.barbarabaileyenterprises.com

www.ingramcontent.com/pod-product-compliance
Lightning Source LLC
Chambersburg PA
CBHW071224170626
46809CB00005BA/1928